The Christmas Tree Angel

By Lisa Soland

With illustrations
by Bethany A. Badeaux

Christmas 2013

To Lilly Family,
Merry Christmas!
Lisa Soland

Jeremiah 29:11

Celtic Cat Publishing
KNOXVILLE, TENNESSEE

Celtic Cat Publishing
2654 Wild Fern Lane
Knoxville, Tennessee 37931
www.celticcatpublishing.net
www.celticcatpublishing.com

Manufactured in the United States of America
Book design and production by Dariel Mayer
Front cover photograph by Lisa Soland
Back cover photograph of Bethany Badeaus by Todd Badeaux

ISBN: 978-0-9891380-5-5

Library of Congress Control Number: 2013943435

I dedicate this book to my parents, my family, Bethel Encino, Chip Chalmers, all the actors who brought these characters to life off the page, and to my husband. You are living proof that when the gift is from the heart, anything is possible.

Introduction
and Acknowledgments

The Christmas Tree Angel was written at Christmas time, just before the turn of the last century. The story was read, as it was being created, chapter-by-chapter to my family who had gathered together to celebrate the birth of Jesus. I am grateful to my parents, and to my brother and his family, for receiving the new words with love and encouragement.

The story was shared again with my husband during our courtship in 2001, but it wasn't until Christmas of 2003 when the promise of a larger audience began to take form. Our friend Chip Chalmers was visiting to celebrate the holiday and requested that we not exchange store-bought gifts. Instead, he played us a beautiful song on his guitar and I read *The Christmas Tree Angel.* Chip was delighted and recommended that we cast the characters from the story and record *The Christmas Tree Angel* as a radio drama.

In August of 2004, cast and crew gathered in the recording studio of the TV show *Scrubs.* With the help of Joe Foglia and Scott Brewster, we put the story on tape. Sound effects were added and the CDs were distributed to the Braille Institute, Starlight Starbright Children's Foundation, and the Los Angeles Children's Hospital. It was director Chip Chalmer's vision to give of our God-given gifts for the benefit of the underprivileged during the holiday. I want to thank him for his graciousness, and all the actors who gave of themselves with no financial reward: Chris Durmick, Andy Eichner, Melanie Ewbank, Julie Maddalena Kliewer, Joe Russell, Brianne Siddall, and Steven L. Sears, who also photographed the event.

The Christmas Tree Angel Radio Drama premiered on December 16, 2004, to a sold out crowd at Bethel church in Encino, California. I would like to personally thank Henry Polic II who debuted the role of the narrator, as well as Joy Kilpatrick, Brian Barnett, Kevin Kruse, my stage manager Vincent Archer, and all the children and behind-the-scenes friends involved in supporting that original production. Theatre is collaborative by nature, and without you, the story simply could not have been told.

The years progressed until I met Jim Johnston of Celtic Cat Publishing. He is a soft-spoken man who helped prepare the angel for her next journey onto the bookshelves and into your homes. I am grateful for his kindness and patience. Also, a special thanks to Bethany Badeaux, the book's illustrator, for her charming and creative images which help bring *The Christmas Tree Angel* to life in a whole new way.

And last but never least, thank you to my husband, who gives his heart to me on a regular basis. I love you, and you all. Thank you.

The Christmas Tree Angel

Chapter 1

The Gift

Once upon a holiday time, in a snow-covered Christmassy town, an ornament was delivered as a gift of good tidings to the Brown family who lived on the hill. The local pastor, upon giving the little angel, gave of his heart as well, and a little more light was in the room than before.

"The merriest of Christmases to you, Mrs. Brown. May this angel bring you and your family peace and protection." He patted her hand and then departed, for the night was blustery and he had many more stops to make.

Mrs. Brown shivered as she closed the door and gathered the hand-knit shawl tightly to her chest. "I don't remember a colder Christmas Eve. I hope we have enough wood for the fire."

Still holding the ornament in her hand, she called to her son. "Tommy! We have a new ornament. One more ornament for the tree."

The boy ran into the room, dressed in his red and green flannel pajamas. Moist chocolate still lingered above his lip. Mrs. Brown smiled at the sight. Hot cocoa was the perfect remedy for a child's anxious Christmas wishes.

"Oh boy, Mom," Tommy exclaimed. "Let me put it on the tree. Here, I'll do it. Let me put it on."

"All right, Tommy. But stop jumping and catch your breath. You'll need to be gentle. This angel is such a special addition to our tree." She placed the delicate ornament into his trembling, little hands and up onto the tree it went, but only as high as Tommy could reach, which was about four feet and two inches.

Mrs. Brown carefully lit each candle on the tree. Together, mother and son stepped back to look at the results of their labor. But how could something this fun be thought of as labor? This was true Christmas spirit. They looked forward to it all year through. Why, it was only this afternoon that the blacksmith had dropped the tree off at their doorstep. Now they gazed at their fully decorated Christmas tree, lit up like a forest of synchronized fireflies.

"Gee, playing with the ornaments sure was fun," Tommy said.

"Doesn't it look lovely?" replied his mother.

"Can we pull them all off and do it again?"

"I don't think so, young man. It's time for you to go to bed."

"Oooohh, Mom. Can't I stay up just a little while longer?" Tommy had cuddled himself around the bottom of the tree and was gazing upward through its scented boughs. He had already secretly examined most of the presents, searching for a special something.

What he really wanted couldn't possibly come in such small, ordinary packages. His perfect present would need to be bolted and screwed together. The wheels would need to be oiled and the red paint shined. A bicycle! He longed for one so dearly. His dreams had him riding on blue-lined clouds every night since his father announced that Christmas was on its way.

"You need to go to bed *now,* honey."

"How 'bout I sleep here under the tree?" He pointed out the exact location he had in mind.

"We've already talked about this, Tommy. It's Christmas Eve and we must give Santa enough time to leave his blessings."

"I was a good boy this year, wasn't I, Mom?"

"Yes, you were, most of the time. Now off you go, young man." Mrs. Brown patted Tommy on his plaid-covered bottom and he scampered down the hall. She smiled once more at the pastor's fine gift, carefully blew out each candle on the tree, and then retired for the evening.

In the still of the night a key turned in the front door. Mr. Brown stepped through the doorway, bundled in layers of warm clothing. He peeled them off as he stood on the welcome mat, knocking the snow from his heavy, black boots.

As he crossed through the room, a flicker of light from the tree caught his eye. "Mrs. Brown! How could she have left a candle burning on the tree," he said to himself. "A sure chance for a fire!" He drew in a breath, ready to blow out the burning light, but there was none. No candle. No flame. Only a Christmas angel ornament he had not seen before. She seemed to be smiling back at him and beaming white light.

Mr. Brown could not put into words why he had to smile while looking at the angel. All he knew was that his heart was glad.

He yawned and then checked in on Tommy. For a moment he watched his son sleeping and was amazed at how fast he was growing into a fine young man. He then knelt beside Tommy's bed and kissed him. "Good night, my precious boy."

Mr. Brown stoked the embers in his own fireplace, in the room he shared with Mrs. Brown. He then tucked himself beneath the warm quilt, cuddled up close to his wife, and fell fast asleep.

Outside, all that could be seen moving on this sleepy night was a thin wisp of smoke rising from each of the three chimneys on the Browns' little home on the hill.

Chapter 2

The Climb

The room with the tree was quiet as the angel recalled the long
carriage ride and being carried into the Browns' home wrapped
in a woolen blanket. She remembered the warmth in the heart of
the man who brought her here. And she remembered a small boy
placing her on the tall tree. She thought of this most of all because
she felt his joy and his hope of things to come.

Her eyes focused as she looked about the tree. Was she alone?
Oh, she couldn't bear being alone after such a long journey. She
turned her stiff neck and caught sight of a clown holding an
orange balloon.

"Hello there, jolly clown," she said. "And how might you be
doing on this fine evening?"

"Oh, I'm jolly enough tonight, but tomorrow's eve will bring
about another painted face on me; one of sorrow and sadness,"
said the clown.

"Why is that?" asked the angel.

"If you don't know, I'm not one to burst your balloon."

"Burst my balloon?" she repeated quietly to herself. His remark
seemed odd. She couldn't imagine life on this tree to be anything
but joyful. She looked to the left, away from the clown, and saw
what seemed to be a wise man dressed in purple velvet.

"And how might you be this evening, wise king?" she asked.

"This night is the best of all nights," said the king, "so I am nothing but delighted. But it means very soon, darkness. Darkness to come."

"Darkness?" asked the angel.

"Yes, darkness. A very long darkness with cold and nothingness for days."

The little angel trembled. No matter which way she turned, she couldn't escape the warning words of darkness. She longed to feel once more the joy of the boy and the gentle touch of his mother. With these pleasant thoughts in her head, she was able to think more clearly.

"I will climb. I will climb up this tree!" she exclaimed. And she began to lift herself, reaching as far as she could, one wing at a time. It was difficult, for sure, but she was determined. She stretched her wings and then pulled some more.

The voices frightened her as she climbed. And if the truth were known, it made the climbing rather difficult.

"It won't make a difference, Miss Angel," cried the king. "No matter how high you climb. It will still come to you."

And if that wasn't enough, a cantankerous lamb, who hung on the tree not far from the others, put in his two bleats as well. "You caaaan't escape the daaaarkness. All of us must faaaace it, and soon."

Their words fell hard upon her ears and caused her painted eyes to water, but her mind was made up. She had chosen to climb. There must be something better on the top of this tree, she thought. At least from there I will be able to see things much clearer.

Of course, wings aren't meant for climbing. They tear and they rip, and so they did on this delicate angel, all the way up the Christmas tree. But, though torn and weary, the little angel was

happy for she was on her way. The angel was now on a journey of her own choosing. "Almost there," she sighed.

The air grew cold in the room as the last bit of wood turned gray. The angel reached and strained for the last time. Somehow, perhaps with the help of holiday spirit, she climbed all the way up to the top of the tree.

And she was right. Things were better here. She felt more comfortable sitting upon fewer boughs. Her white satin dress lay as it should, in a complete circle without bunching up.

"Why, this is where I was meant to be all along," said the angel. "I belong on the *top* of the Christmas tree." A smile returned to her painted face. "What a journey I've had. What a very long journey."

Much to her dismay, there was little left of her wings. Though the wire that held them fast to their form was still in place, the finely woven lace had suffered significant damage. Pieces hung hopelessly. Although the angel had never considered flight, the idea now seemed impossible.

But she wasn't going to think of such things. Not now. She was too tired to face any more peril. It was time to rest. So, the little angel wrapped a branch around her midriff and quickly fell asleep.

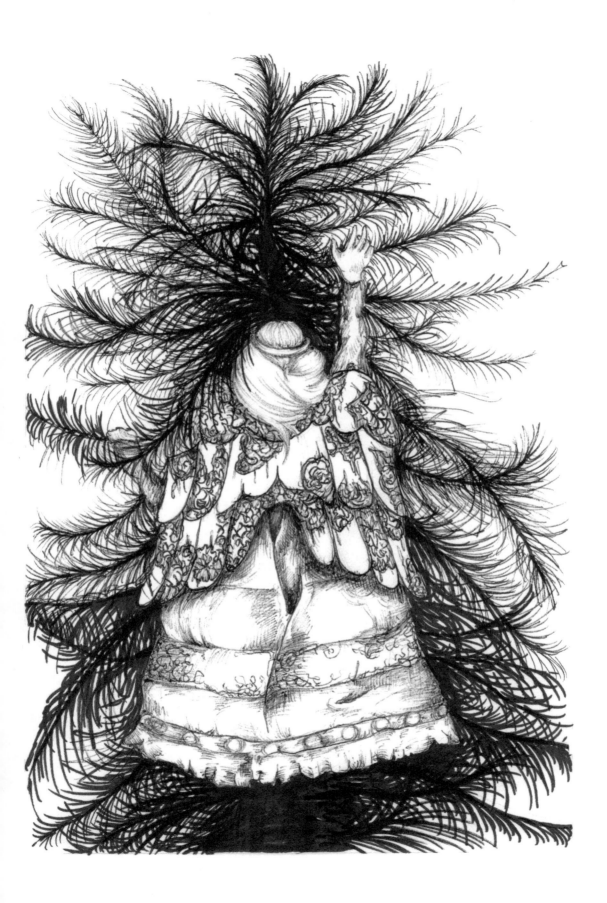

Chapter 3

Tommy's Present

Christmas morning seems to come the slowest of all mornings. The darkness of night refuses to change, as if the entire world is closed inside of a cardboard box. But come it did, as all mornings do. Tommy was up and bouncing as the sun cast its rays into the room and onto the tree. He screamed with delight when he spotted the red bike parked between the fireplace and the front door. A large green bow covered the silver handlebars.

"Oh my gosh! I got it. I got my bike. Yippee!"

As quickly as he appeared, Tommy was gone again, sliding his way across the hardwood floor on his way to wake up his mom and dad. His voice echoed through the halls, "I got it. Santa left me a bike. Can I ride it? Can I ride it now, before breakfast, Mom?"

There was a moment of silence in the Browns' home. Two sleepy adults with tousled hair appeared in robes. Tommy dragged them toward his newfound treasure. "Look, Mom. Look, Pop. I must have been a very good boy. Look what Santa left me."

With eyes half opened, Mrs. Brown veered off to the kitchen. "I'll put on the coffee," she mumbled.

Mr. Brown ran a hand through his hair and then cleared his throat. "Now Tommy, Santa gave you this bike in hopes that you would be careful with it."

"I will, Pop."

"Listen to me, Son."

"I am."

"A bike like this is a little tougher to ride than that old tricycle of yours."

"I know, Pop. I'll be careful."

"Your mom or I need to be with you when you ride, especially when you're first starting out."

"Sure, Pop. I know," said Tommy, growing bored with the drill.

Just then, Mrs. Brown reappeared in the doorway. "I'm worried about him, honey. We live on a hill and that will make it hard for him to learn."

"I'll take it to the park, Mom. I'll walk my bike down the hill to the park and ride it there."

"We'll talk about this some more later," said Mrs. Brown. "For now, how about we all sit down to some nice. . ."

Mr. Brown interrupted. "What is that you're cooking in there, Mrs. Brown? Fried eggs?"

"Yes, fried eggs and porridge," smiled Mrs. Brown.

"Well, that sounds mighty fine," he said. "And then we've more presents to open." The three of them left the room. Tommy walked backwards so he could watch his new, shiny red bike as long as he possibly could.

The room once again grew silent.

Chapter 4

A New Friend

The branches on most trees tend to thin out toward the top. This is the very reason fewer ornaments are hung there. From this spot, her spot, the little angel had the pleasure of witnessing her first Christmas morning. How blessed she was to experience the pure joy of a child's heart. Happiness filled her completely. Today was a brand new day. But as soon as she found herself happy, the thought came that she was alone. She turned her face to the left and then to the right and noticed there was no one near. She had climbed herself right into loneliness.

"Hello there." The angel heard a strong and kind voice. "Good morning and Merry Christmas."

It must be coming from below her feet somewhere.

"Can you hear me?" the voice asked.

The angel thought of looking down, but the idea frightened her. In fact, it made her tremble though the voice seemed pleasant.

"I said, up there. Can you hear me?"

The angel replied, "Why, yes. Yes, I can."

"I'm a bit below you. Over here, to the right."

"Oh, my!" exclaimed the angel.

"It's all right. You're anchored rather well on that sturdy branch. Take a chance and look at me," said the voice.

The angel certainly thought the chance was worth taking for she could surely use a friend. She stretched her neck as far as she could and sure enough, at the base of her gown, a little over to the right hung a soldier. Quite handsome in his appearance, she thought. And he looked up at her, smiling.

"Well, good morning and Merry Christmas to you," he said.

The colors he wore were not freshly painted reds and blues as you might think. They were worn and faded. But like his voice, the soldier's face was strong and kind.

"Merry Christmas to *you*," said the angel timidly. As she gazed at him, her cheeks grew quite warm.

"You're a genuine sight for sore eyes," said the soldier.

"Who, me?"

"Is there any other angel up there on the top of this tree?" asked the soldier playfully.

"Why, no. There isn't. I suppose I'm it."

"In all my life I've never seen an ornament change their position as much as you," said the soldier, rather impressed. "In fact, besides me, no ornament has ever moved from the position in which they were originally placed."

"Really?" asked the angel, not at all aware of her accomplishment.

"Certainly not. And it's a good thing. What would the family think if they came back into the room and none of the ornaments were where they put them?"

"I suppose you're right."

"I most certainly am. Everyone stays in their place because they're afraid to do anything other than what is expected of them. They never even suspect they *can* move themselves about," he said. "But I hear a lot of wishing going on."

"Wishing? What kind of wishing?" asked the angel.

"Oh, your basic ornament wishes like, 'I wish Mrs. Brown would come along and move us somewhere else.' Or, 'Gee, I wish

Tommy was a tad taller. He hears us when we talk and he could put us wherever we want to go.'"

"The boy can hear us?" the angel asked.

"Yes, he can now but that will come to an end in another year or two."

"I see."

"That was quite a climb last night," said the soldier.

"Yes, and I've a little less lace for it, I'm afraid."

"Well, no worry. Mrs. Brown will mend you before she puts you away for the year."

"Away for the year?"

"Oh, yes," he nodded. "Mr. Brown is deathly afraid of a fire with the candles burning on the tree. So, tonight's the night. The old grandfather clock in the hall will strike six and the Brown family will begin to take down the Christmas tree. All of us ornaments will be placed back into our boxes and stored in the attic until next year."

At that moment, Tommy reappeared and started to examine the rest of the packages under the tree. His father trailed behind with more wood to add to the fire. Soon, warmth filled the room again. Mrs. Brown joined them, and together they unwrapped the presents and shouted and laughed.

All the while, thoughts spun inside the little angel's head. Could this be true? Is it possible there is no use for me except for these two days a year? Is this the fate that awaits me? It didn't seem possible. An ornament filled with such love to give and no place to give it but to the inside of a box. What kind of a life is that?

She had so much to ask the soldier, who looked like he was enjoying the morning festivities. Had he actually lived through this dreary darkness? How could he bear it? How could he simply hang there on the tree, smiling, knowing what was to come? Buried alive. She was going to be buried alive.

The little angel had worked herself into such an anxious state that she almost shook herself right off the top of the tree when she heard another voice. "Honey, did you move the angel to the top of the tree?" Mrs. Brown asked her husband. The angel froze fast in place.

"No, I did not," said Mr. Brown. "Where did she come from, anyway? I noticed her last night."

"Pastor Nelson paid us a visit yesterday. He brought the angel to us. Isn't she lovely?"

"She looks especially good at the top of the tree," said Mr. Brown. "Very fitting for an angel, wouldn't you say? She can keep an eye on things from up there."

Mrs. Brown smiled. It must have been Mr. Brown who moved the little angel to the top of the tree and now he was playing a joke on her. She leaned over on the sofa and kissed him, softly. "You are a beautiful man, Mr. Brown. And I am so blessed."

Together, they looked at all the opened gifts beneath the tree. "So many toys could keep a young boy busy for a good, long time, Mrs. Brown."

"I think you're probably right, Mr. Brown."

After such a busy morning, Mr. and Mrs. Brown retired to their room. All that could be heard was the sound of wheels pushing against the hardwood floor.

Chapter 5

The Invitation

Tommy's mind raced. Thoughts dashed every which way. He was overwhelmed. The new bike was all he could think of until now, but to have all these other toys, too.

"This truck is great. Look at this. You push it hard into the ground three times and then see. It magically goes all on its own."

And so it did. In fact, the truck rode itself right into the side of Tommy's new bike.

"Wow, this is great. Look at this bike. A basket for newspapers, and a bell too that rings and everything. Did you see this bell?"

The angel wondered to whom the boy was speaking. She whispered to the soldier, "Who is he talking to?"

"I'm talking to you," said the boy, calling to her from the ground. The eyebrows on the little angel practically lifted right off her wooden face.

"To me?" she asked.

"Yes, you. Did you see my new bike this morning? Did you notice how it shines?"

The angel took a long breath. This was an amazing world. She'd never had the company of a child. She'd missed a precious experience and never knew it. After another deep breath, the angel answered the boy. "Yes," she said, "of course I noticed."

"Don't you like my bike, Angel?" the boy asked.

"It's a beautiful bike. You've certainly been blessed."

"Yes. I am the most blessed boy on the hill."

"But not so blessed to live on a hill," said the angel.

"Oh, you heard that?" asked Tommy with sadness in his voice. "You heard my mom and dad?"

"They seem to be very concerned about you," she said. "They must love you very much."

"I guess so," shrugged Tommy as he cranked the bell. The jingling sound excited him all over again. "Look at these handlebars. I can't wait to ride it down the road. I'll be the best newspaper boy in town." He jumped onto the white, leather seat and using his foot to balance, half peddled his way around the room.

Tommy made three full turns and then dismounted. He tried to lower the kickstand but it was hard to budge for such a small boy. Instead, he leaned the bike against the stone of the fireplace. "Angel, how did you get up to the top of our Christmas tree?" he asked. "Did my pop move you there?"

"No. I climbed up, all through the night."

"You must be tired."

"I am," she said.

"Are you having a nice Christmas?" Tommy asked. "What did you get?"

"Oh, my. What did I get?" The angel smiled. "Why, I got you, Tommy."

"Me?" This made Tommy very happy though he hadn't a clue why.

"Yes, you."

"Gee. What do you know about that? I gave you a Christmas present and I didn't even know it." His heart glowed warmly beneath his flannel pajamas. "Fly down here, Angel. I want to give you a ride on my new bike."

Could he have said what she thought he said? The angel leaned forward and asked him politely to repeat himself.

"I said fly down here. My parents are sleeping and I'd like to give you a ride on my new bike."

The angel's head spun. Was this possible? Could she really leap off this tree?

"I'd take you down myself but I'm only this high." He held up his hand as tall as the hair on his head to prove to the angel how impossible that task would be. "Quick, hop off. I'll catch you. Here, look. I'll use my new baseball glove." In no time flat, Tommy had the leather glove out of the box and onto his left hand. "I was first baseman last summer. My pop gave me this for my very own. It's big so I can catch better. Neat, huh?"

The angel thought perhaps she was dreaming. Maybe she imagined this better future to avoid the one described to her by the other ornaments. She blinked her eyes repeatedly to force herself awake.

"Are you coming or not?" Tommy asked impatiently.

The angel whispered to her friend, the good soldier, "What should I do?"

"What do you want to do?" he whispered back.

"My wings. They're torn. They won't work. I've ripped them." Her voice cracked with emotion. "I'll do nothing but fall."

"Well, you could stay and hope that we are put into the same box together," said the soldier. "The ornaments hung close to one another usually end up in the same box."

The same box. The words echoed in her ears. The same box, the same darkness, the same cold. What kind of a life is that? Even next to a friend, it's still darkness.

"Why don't you come with me?" she said to the soldier.

"No."

"Why not? Come with me."

"That sounds doubly risky, don't you think?"

"So you don't think I can make it?"

"Angel, I believe you can do anything you put your mind to."

"But what about my wings?"

"They may surprise you."

The angel closed her eyes, took a deep breath, and turned back to Tommy. She was ready to jump, but he was gone. She'd taken too long to decide and so had lost her chance. If she had a heart beneath the pearl necklace and the satin dress and the carefully carved wood, it was breaking. It was breaking within her.

"Don't worry, pretty angel. He'll be back," said the soldier, who was now right beside her. He had climbed up the rest of the way to comfort her, and now they stood side by side at the top of the tree.

"He'll be back," the soldier said again. "You'll see."

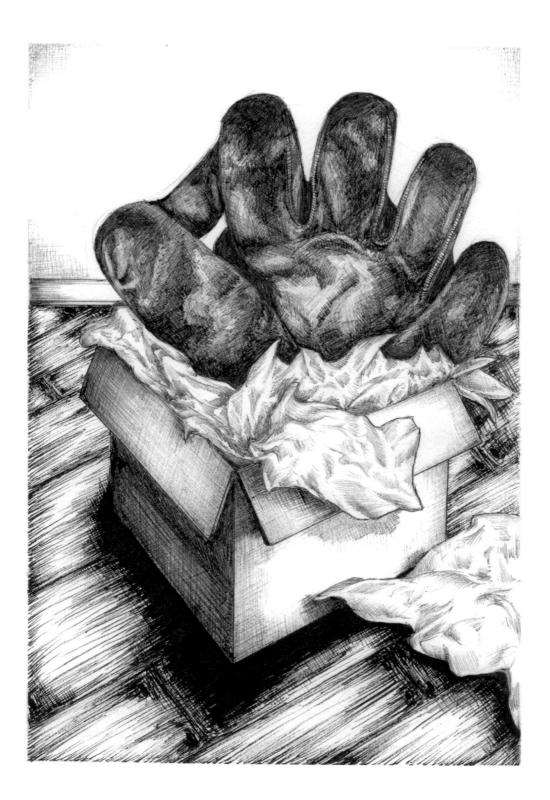

Chapter 6

Off to Grandma's

The sun had now become a part of the afternoon sky. The room with the tree took on a different shade of light. With the angel's hand in his, the soldier spoke to her of his many adventures as they passed the slow hours of Christmas. Their exchanges differed from others that day. They gave to each other gifts of storytelling and careful listening and the comfort of a held hand.

In the simplicity of this setting, Tommy bound in anew wearing his Sunday best and looking for something fun to do.

"Tommy, your galoshes are in the window seat," called Mrs. Brown who was roasting something wonderful in the kitchen. The smells of the delicious food filled the small home on the hill.

"I don't want to go," Tommy said to himself under his breath.

But Mr. Brown entered just in time to catch Tommy's words that were meant only for the walls and maybe the listening ornaments.

"The choice is not for you to make, Son," he said.

Tommy hung his head. "I know, Pop."

"Apologize and put on your overcoat."

"I'm sorry." Tommy reluctantly pulled on the plain, rubber boots but let the top to the window seat slam shut.

"Tommy."

"Oops. And I'm sorry for that too," he added.

"I'll help your mother with the turkey." Mr. Brown left the room.

Tommy called after him, "Pop, can I take my bike to Grandma's?"

"No, Son."

"How 'bout something smaller?"

"Pocket size," Mr. Brown yelled. "Bring something that can fit into your pocket."

This left Tommy to wonder what Santa gave him that could possibly fit into the pocket of his woolly coat. There was the yellow dump truck that drove itself. There was the mitt and the bike. But no, the bike had already been discussed.

Pocket size! Tommy thought hard as he looked about the room. The hoop and stick certainly didn't qualify. "Why is it that only impossible tasks are asked of me?" he asked himself.

Tommy reached into his pocket and imagined the possibilities. It was rather deep and wide compared to his small, mittened hand. Why, you could fit an apple pie in there if you weren't afraid of losing the filling. "That's a mighty big pocket," he exclaimed. He then looked to the top of the tree. "Angel, what are you planning for this afternoon?" After a moment of waiting, the boy called out again. "Angel, are you awake?"

Just then Mr. and Mrs. Brown came into the room carrying the turkey and a pecan pie wrapped up and ready for travel. "Thank you for dressing so quickly, Tommy," said Mrs. Brown.

"What gift did you decide to bring, Son?" asked Mr. Brown.

Tommy pulled one of the largest red and white candy canes off the Christmas tree. "Is this okay, Mom?"

"Yes, Tommy. But make sure you wait until after you've finished your Christmas dinner."

The Browns' bundled themselves up and opened the front door inviting in such a wind that the snowflake ornaments could no longer hold on to the tree. They blew out the front door,

danced their way across the lawn, and played happily atop the real snowflakes of winter.

Inside, the angel and the soldier had arranged several solid branches to lie on and had fallen fast asleep, still gently holding each other's hands as they napped. Sharing their captivating lives had brought them closer. Amongst all the newness of a busy world, they had found comfort in each other. No sounds from below could have disturbed them.

The tree was silent, and so was the home on the hill on this white Christmassy afternoon.

Chapter 7

A Surprise Visit

Sometimes things you want to do are quickly followed by things you don't want to do. And so the cycle continues. For this is how living things grow—by work of both the sun and the snow. The Brown family returned home for the evening with Tommy's candy cane half eaten and Mr. Brown's belt loosened another notch. The cool air from the opened door brushed across the angel's face, waking her from her nap.

"How about you play some Christmas music on that new Victrola of yours, Mrs. Brown?" suggested her husband, "and we'll all change into some comfortable clothes to take down the tree."

Father and son left the room, itching to get out of their wool suits. Mrs. Brown took a rare moment for herself and fondly gazed upon the tree for the last time. "If it were left to me, I'd leave you up all season long. It seems a shame to limit Christmas spirit to these two days a year."

Mrs. Brown's words echoed in the angel's ears as if she'd dreamed them. *It seems a shame to limit Christmas spirit to these two days a year.*

"Soldier. Soldier, wake up. The family is home, and I'm afraid."

The soldier held the angel's hand a bit tighter and said, "Somehow I know everything's going to be fine."

"What time is it?" asked the angel.

"There's no way of knowing until the sounds come from the hall."

"The grandfather clock?"

"Yes. That's right."

This strong and kind soldier continued to comfort her, but the thought of what was to come did not. The angel trembled with no answers for the trial she was about to face.

"Maybe we could climb down," she said.

"There's no time for that now. It took you all night to climb up half way. Remember?"

"Yes, but going down must be easier."

"You wouldn't make it."

"Don't you mean, *we*? *We* wouldn't make it?"

The soldier was silent.

"If there was a way to fix my wings, maybe we could fly. What do you think my soldier?"

"He thinks you taaaalk too much," bleated the lamb from below.

Then something stirred from the other side of the tree. A camel, with one hump and four long legs appeared. "Well, hi there, you two," said the slow speaking camel. "I've been listening to your dilemma."

"Who haaaasn't?" bleated the lamb.

Both the soldier and the angel didn't know what to say. What a surprise. Another ornament had joined them at the top of the tree.

"It took me all afternoon but I finally got here. I think I might be the solution to your problem," said the camel.

"If it took you all afternoon to climb around the side of this tree, how might you be the solution?" asked the soldier.

"Haven't you ever heard of camel hair coats?"

"Why, yes. Everyone's heard of camel hair coats," said the angel. "But I don't need a coat."

"What she could use is a pair of wings. Do you happen to have a spare set in your saddlebags there?" asked the soldier, losing his patience.

"Camel coats are made with camel hair. My hair. Why don't you use my hair to mend your wings?"

Truth is obvious when a mind is clear, and the soldier's mind cleared at once. "Now that might work!" he exclaimed.

The moment their plan was set in motion, the grandfather clock in the hall began to chime. The three ornaments looked at each other, each holding his breath. Not one of them moved a single thread. The soldier, at last, broke the silence. "It could be only five o'clock."

"Or it could be only four," said the camel.

"Well, you were awake, Camel. Did the clock already chime four or five?" asked the soldier.

"I don't know," said the camel. "I can only count to two."

So it was past two o'clock and before six. That much they knew. If it was after six, the Browns would have taken down the tree and the ornaments would already be in darkness.

The grandfather clock struck three as the ornaments held their positions on the tree. The silence between the chimes seemed endless. Then the fourth sound rang out from the hall. The angel wondered why she had never noticed these deafening noises before.

"Let's make some popcorn, Mom."

"Oh, Tommy, we've just had dinner. Aren't you full from dinner?"

"No. See? I've got lots of room." He pulled the top of his trousers away from his belly to prove his point. "It's Christmas Day, Mom. There's a lot of room for wishes to still come true."

"Yes, I think you're right, Tommy," said Mrs. Brown. "Let's make some popcorn."

"Yippee. Thanks, Mom." Tommy slid his way down the hall.

The human voices filled the moments between the fourth and the fifth chime. But the longest pause of all was the one that came after the fifth. It was so long, in fact, that the angel, the soldier, and the camel thought the sixth sound would not come at all. But it did. Oh, but it did.

Chapter 8

The Plan

"I could haaaave told you it was six o'clock," said the lamb from below. "But you haaaad to draaaag it out, didn't you?"

"Listen," said the solider to his friends. "The Browns decorate the tree the same way every year, from the top to the bottom. But they un-decorate it exactly opposite of that, from the bottom to the top. That should buy us some time. Let's get to work and see how far we can get."

"I'm game," said the camel. He then jokingly added, "But don't shoot me."

They all smiled at the camel's attempt at humor, and then with a nod from the angel, they began. The soldier pulled out one hair at a time from the coat of the camel. "Ouch." And then he used it to tie together the shredded lace of the angel's wings. Each time he pulled out a strand, the camel let out an, "Ouch." So the soldier pulled, and the camel "ouched." And on they went.

And the Brown family appeared, one by one into the room with the tree. It seemed to be three against three, a race against time.

"Ouch."

As Mrs. Brown cleared the presents from beneath the tree, she spotted her holiday record, a gift from Mr. Brown. Her husband cranked up the Victrola, she placed the needle on the spinning groove, and the song rang out into the air: *Hark, the herald angels sing, "Glory to the newborn King."* Although this song spoke of cheer, declaring peace on Earth and mercy mild, the angel felt no peace in

37

her heart. All she felt was dread of the inescapable: the box, the attic, and days upon days of darkness and nothingness and fear.

"Faster. Faster," encouraged the angel, though her friends were already going as fast as they could.

They had repaired one wing and were moving onto the next when the dreaded boxes were dragged into the room, scraping loudly against the hardwood floor. At the sight of them, the angel shook, which made tying knots on her wings even more difficult.

"Please stop shaking," pleaded the solider, who was doing the very best he could.

The camel thought talking about something pleasant might calm the angel. "I've been with the Brown family for nearly twelve years now."

The soldier understood what the camel was doing and joined in. "Oh, really!" he added.

"Oh, yes," said the camel. "True story. I was tied to the top of a wedding present."

"Were the Browns married on Christmas Day?" asked the soldier.

"Christmas Eve, and I saw the entire ceremony from up here, on the tree. Quite moving, actually," said the camel. "I was quite moved."

"Are you tying?" cried out the angel, who was doing her very best, too.

"We're moving right along," said the camel. "No fret. No fret. Right along. Ouch." The camel tried hard to be cheerful but Mrs. Brown and Tommy were already half way up the tree.

"You know," bleated the lamb. "Even if you turkeys maaaake it off this tree, you're still going to eeeend up in the boooox." Right then, the lamb himself was plucked from his temporary home amongst the branches. Tommy asked him, "Don't you ever have anything good to say, Lamb?"

"Very nice weather we're haaaaving, don't you think?" he said, and into the box he went.

The wise man was next to go. "The happiest of New Years to you, Tommy, my boy."

"Why thank you, King. And a very happy New Year to you, too."

"Who are you talking to, Tommy?" asked Mrs. Brown.

"The ornaments," said Tommy.

"The ornaments?"

"Yup."

The three workers at the top of the tree stopped to listen. Mrs. Brown took the record off the Victrola.

"They tell me how they're feeling and where they want to go on the tree," said Tommy.

"And how long has this been going on?" asked his mother.

"Uhhhmmm. As long as I can remember," answered Tommy, who thought his mother had reacted strangely to a simple exchange of words.

Mrs. Brown wondered how she should handle this. She and Mr. Brown encouraged Tommy to have his own thoughts, and creativity was always welcome in their little home on the hill, but she wasn't sure about talking to ornaments. This might be something to share with Mr. Brown, she thought. Two minds stand a better chance at choosing the right way to go.

"Honey?" she called out to her husband.

"I'm in here, making cocoa," he answered from down the hall.

"Tommy, why don't you play with your toys for a bit? I'll go help your father in the kitchen."

"Okay, Mom. I can't reach any more ornaments by myself anyway."

Chapter 9

True Purpose

Tommy dropped down on his knees and ran the yellow truck across the hardwood floor. The camel, the soldier, and the angel went back to work, moving faster than ever. Tommy had borrowed them some time.

"Ouch."

"Sorry," said the soldier.

"Ouch."

"Sorry."

"Ouch."

"Sorry!"

"What are you three doing up there?" Tommy called up to them. The ornaments froze fast in place. "What's wrong, Angel? Why aren't you talking with me anymore?"

"Tommy," she said. "I'm having my wings fixed."

"Ouch," said the camel, as quietly as he could.

"What's wrong with them?" Tommy asked.

"They ripped apart while I was climbing to the top of the tree."

"I'm sorry," said Tommy. "Does it hurt much?"

"Ouch," murmured the camel.

"Not for me, but I'm afraid the camel might be a little worse for wear."

"Oh, I don't mind," said the camel. "Happy to give. Happy to give. Ouch."

"Quite honestly, I'm glad to be whole again, Tommy," said the angel.

"My mom's in the kitchen. She's talking with my dad about me talking to you."

"What do you think about that?" asked the angel.

"I think maybe I'm in trouble," said Tommy.

"Oh, I wouldn't want that," said the angel, concerned for the boy.

"No, me neither. That's about the only thing I'm afraid of," said Tommy. "What are you afraid of, Angel?"

"Boxes," she said. "I'm afraid of dark places and not being able to love." Admitting her fear out loud seemed like the biggest risk of all.

"Actually, I don't like dark places either. My mom and dad let me keep the door open when I go to bed at night."

"That must be wonderful."

"Yes, it is," said Tommy. "Why don't you fly down here, Angel, and I'll keep you from the dark, too."

Oh those words. Those beautiful words. Could she receive the gift of a second chance? She hoped and longed for the comfort of Tommy's care and a life beyond the box.

The solider whispered to her, "Ask him how. Go ahead. Ask him."

The angel wondered why her friend the solider was having her ask this, but she had learned to trust him. "Tommy," she said. "How will you keep me from the box?"

"I don't know," he answered. "I guess I'll tell my mom and dad that you're afraid."

The solider whispered to the angel, "That won't work. They'll think he's making it up and they'll discourage it."

"You'll end up in the box then, for sure," added the camel, quietly.

"I have an idea," said Tommy. "Why don't you fly down here and I'll put you on the handlebars of my bike." He skipped over to the red flying machine and squeezed the metal lever on the bell to confirm his invitation.

"But what would be my purpose?" asked the angel. "I'm afraid I'll need a purpose, something other than simply sitting on the top of Christmas trees."

"Well" thought Tommy out loud, "I think purposes have something to do with what a person does best. What is it you do best, Angel?"

That was a very difficult question. She remembered the pastor who brought her here and how he offered her in the hope that she would bring peace and protection to the family.

"Tommy," called out the angel. "I have it. I will protect you on your bike, through all your journeys."

"That's good. Mom and Pop will like that. Come on now, before they come back."

The little Christmas angel quivered with happiness. She could both escape the box and do what she did best: protect and serve. Her heart, the one she most certainly had, leapt for joy inside her.

But as quickly as she felt such great happiness, she thought of her friends standing beside her on the tree. Would her new journey include them or would they suffer the fate she had feared? "What will you do, Camel? Will you join me?"

"Oh, no. Not me. I look forward to the long winter's nap. Besides, I have to grow my coat back." He smiled a funny, crooked smile then kissed the angel's rosy cheek. "This is my home and has been for a very long time. I'm comfortable here."

"And my soldier what will you do? Have you made up your mind?" asked the angel, afraid of losing him most of all.

"You know, I've never really found my home. And I never really thought of looking anywhere else until I met you, my angel."

This made her smile, though it was not the answer she'd hoped to hear from his painted mouth.

"So yes," he said. "I will come with you. I suppose I should keep looking for my home until I find it." The angel threw her wings around the soldier's wooden neck.

"Oh. Thank you. Thank you so much," said the angel. And knowing that a very little boy was waiting for them, they paused no longer. The soldier took the angel's hand tightly into his, and together they leapt off the very top of the Browns' Christmas tree.

Chapter 10

Faith

Now this was one, incredible spectacle, let me tell you—two Christmas ornaments with faces fully beaming, soaring mid-air for they were free. Actually, free falling was more like it. No one expected this. Of course, the angel didn't really know if her wings worked or not because they had never been put to the test. But even if they did work, they were probably meant to carry the angel alone, not the soldier too. Much to their dismay, gravity was pulling them faster and faster toward the hardwood floor.

This is the very reason why baseball teams spring up all over small towns like this—so little boys can catch falling ornaments off the top of Christmas trees. Tommy simply moved his arm out from behind him and on his left hand was his beloved glove. He caught them both softly and safely in his padded mitt.

And as he promised, Tommy tied the angel to the handlebars of his bike, right next to the bell. And because he knew of the soldier's fondness for her, he placed him in the wire basket, right next to where he imagined the newspapers would go. The three went for such a ride, around in circles through the room with the tree.

The camel chuckled. "You look like a silly circus act riding in those circles."

They laughed at the sheer wonderfulness of it all. What an accomplishment this was for them. It was quite lovely, until Mr.

and Mrs. Brown stepped back into the room. Mr. Brown looked and sounded very serious. "We need to talk with you, Son."

"Okay, Pop." Tommy brought his bike to a halt as his heart pounded in his chest.

"Your mother tells me that you've been talking with these ornaments."

"Yes, Father." Tommy only called him *Father* when he knew he was in trouble.

Suddenly, Mrs. Brown, seeing the angel perched on the front of the bike, interrupted him, "Tommy, how did the angel get down from the top of the tree?"

Tommy wondered if he should tell the truth. The angel wondered if she'd be boxed. And the soldier stood by simply amazed by it all.

"That angel," said Mrs. Brown, "was at the top of the tree when I left this room."

"Yes. I know, Mother."

"Well, how did she get down from there?"

"I told her to jump, and she did."

There was silence in the room with the tree in the Browns' home on the hill.

"You told her to jump," repeated Tommy's mother. Having no more words, she turned to her husband and said, "There is no way Tommy could have gotten that angel down from the top of that tree."

"I didn't, Mom. She jumped. And I caught her with my glove. See?" Tommy smiled as he showed his parents the baseball glove on his left hand as proof to his heroism.

Mr. Brown, confused as to what to do, looked to his wife for help, but she whispered, "I have faith in you, Mr. Brown."

"Thank you, Mrs. Brown." He cleared his throat. "Son, even

parents sometimes must have faith in things we cannot see or hear. Do you understand what I'm saying, Tommy?"

"Yes, Father. You can't hear the ornaments so you're trying to have faith."

Surprised at his son's young-hearted wisdom, he continued, "Yes, that's right. Now you can see my problem. If what you're telling us is true, why then is it that the ornaments on the tree talk to you but not to us?"

"Because Father, you stopped listening long ago."

Mr. Brown, in that moment, remembered his own boyhood Christmas tree and how he, too, would sleep cuddled up beneath it so he would have a friend to talk to on Christmas Eve. He had forgotten all about his friends on the tree and also the importance of good conversation, sharing, and most importantly—listening. Listening carefully to those you love.

Mr. Brown looked at the angel on Tommy's handlebars. She seemed to be smiling back at him and beaming white light. And though he still could not put into words why he had to smile while looking at the little angel, he was glad. And that was enough. "Tommy?"

"Yes, Pop?"

"That angel sure is a special angel." He turned to his wife. "Isn't she, Mrs. Brown?"

"She sure is," said Mrs. Brown.

"And furthermore, I think we should keep her around all year through."

"Oh, Pop." Tommy threw his arms around his father's neck. "She *is* special, and she's going to protect me on my bike. She said so."

"Well now, that's a worry off my mind," said Mrs. Brown. "And what about this ornament here, Son? What about this soldier?" she asked, noticing the soldier standing at attention in the basket of the bike.

"Well, the two of them are good friends so they have to stay together."

Mr. and Mrs. Brown couldn't help but smile at their son. Tommy reminded them of the most important things in life—love and friendship and staying together.

And so they did—the angel and the soldier and Tommy. They stayed together all year through, every year. And Tommy learned how to ride that two-wheeled bicycle safely, like it had been born beneath him, which pleased his pop. They rode to the park, to church on Sundays, and even down the hill on which the Browns' home stood.

Tommy no longer feared getting into trouble. The angel no longer feared being put in a box. And the soldier found his home amongst his true friends.

It isn't every day an angel is given as a gift of good tidings but, when the gift is from the heart, anything is possible.

And so it was in the Browns' home on the hill. Like that first Christmas long ago, miracles reside in the smallest of places, and sometimes in the littlest of angels.

ABOUT CELTIC CAT PUBLISHING

Celtic Cat Publishing was founded in 1995 to publish emerging and established writers. The following works are available from Celtic Cat Publishing at *www.celticcatpublishing.net*, *Amazon.com*, and major bookstores.

Regional	*Appalachian Tales & Heartland Adventures*, Bill Landry
	Tellin' It for the Truth, Bill Landry
Poetry	*The Ghost in the Word: Poems*, Arthur J. Stewart
	Exile Revisited, James B. Johnston
	Revelations: Poems, Ted Olson
	Marginal Notes, Frank Jamison
	Rough Ascension and Other Poems of Science, Arthur J. Stewart
	Bushido: The Virtues of Rei and Makoto, Arthur J. Stewart
	Circle, Turtle, Ashes, Arthur J. Stewart
	Ebbing & Flowing Springs, Jeff Daniel Marion
	Gathering Stones, KB Ballentine
	Fragments of Light, KB Ballentine
	Guardians, Laura Still
Fiction	*The Price of Peace*, James B. Johnston
	Outpost Scotland, Abbott A. Brayton
Humor	*Life Among the Lilliputians*, Judy Lockhart DiGregorio
	Memories of a Loose Woman, Judy Lockhart DiGregorio
	Jest Judy (CD), Judy Lockhart DiGregorio
Chanukah	*One for Each Night: Chanukah Tales and Recipes*, Marilyn Kallet
Young Adult	*Voyage of Dreams: An Irish Memory*, Kathleen E. Fearing
Children	*Buddy: Dog of the Smoky Mountains*, Ryan Webb and Sharon Poole
	Jack the Healing Cat (English), Marilyn Kallet
	Jacques le chat guérisseur (French), Marilyn Kallet
	Twins, Tracy Ryder Bradshaw
Memoir	*Being Alive*, Raymond Johnston
Philosophy	*The Epiphany of K*, Kenneth Godwin